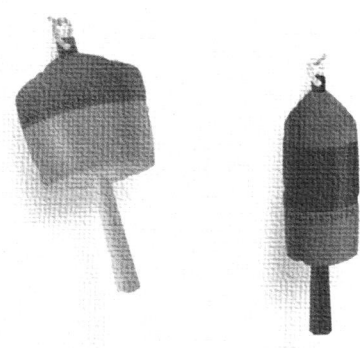

This Book
Belongs To-

Boat & Wind

Written by Steve Tiller

Illustrated by Robert Cremeans

MichaelsMind®
ATLANTA

SM

Steve Tiller, Author
Robert Cremeans, Illustrator / Creative Director
Kathryn L. Tecosky, Editor
Mary Huggins, Grammarian

Special thanks to: Our Families, CCAD, The Chicago Bromleys, David & Melissa Abbey, Alan at CopyCraft,
and Brian Bias our Apple guru.

Library of Congress Cataloging-in-Publication Data
Tiller, Steve

Summary:
The story of a small boat that discovers that faith fills his sails with power and purpose as he
explores the friendship he develops with the warm summer wind.

ISBN 0-9704597-8-5
[1. Sailboat - Children's Fiction.   2. Ocean - Fiction.   3. Boat - Faith]

Printed by
Daehan Printing in South Korea

Illustrations in this book were created on a Macintosh G4 computer using Adobe Photoshop and a mouse!

Visit us for fun and games at:
www.michaelsmind.com

To the Spirit of Truth, and to Living Faith; may we all explore
the great ocean of life with a grateful heart and an open mind.

-S.T.

To my Wind with love!   -R.C.

Once there was a sailboat who was a friend of the wind. Each day the little boat and the wind talked and played together as they skimmed along the bright blue sea.

"Yahoo! I love crashing into waves," laughed the boat, "the spray goes everywhere!"

"I know," puffed the wind as a quick breeze shot the little boat toward another wave.

When the boat laughed the wind was happy. The wind loved the little boat.

"You should see the sunlight dance on the water," giggled the little boat.

"I do see it," breezed the wind.

"I'd like to see you sometimes," said the boat.

"I know," whispered the wind.

The happy boat lived in a harbor where the river met the sea. At the end of each day the wind carried the boat back home. At night the sailboat shared his feelings with the wind, and the wind whispered his thoughts of joy to the boat.

"I loved the ocean today with its great waves. It was like climbing up mountains and sliding down the other side. It was a roller coaster ride!"

"I know," said the wind, "I was there too."

"You know, some of the boats think you aren't real."

"Some of them do talk like that," sighed the wind.

"It's hard to believe in things you can't see," added the sailboat thoughtfully.

"Just because you can't see me doesn't mean I am not here!"

As time passed, the sailboat wanted to be like some of the other boats and he stopped talking to the wind. And soon, the little boat stopped believing he had ever talked to the wind.

The wind, however, did not forget the little boat. He loved the boat and believed in him. Each day he blew his breezy breath until the sails of the boat were fat and full, and the little boat would go skimming across the waves of the sea.

The sailboat spent each day doing what sailboats do. He sailed. But something seemed to be missing for the little boat. He did not enjoy crashing the waves to make the salty sea spray high in the air anymore. The sea did not sparkle in the sun the way it did. The boat did not seem to laugh as much.

He tried to make friends with the other boats, but boats mostly just keep to themselves. The little sailboat knew something was wrong, but he couldn't remember exactly what it was. So he just kept sailing and sailing and sailing.

One day the little boat sailed very far out into the deep blue sea. It was further than he had ever sailed from land. The boat followed the waves up and down all day. Finally toward evening, the boat turned to go back to the harbor but there was no land in sight.

The sailboat had a sinking feeling. He came about and looked in the other direction, but there was still no land. The boat turned around again and again. All he could see was water. There was no land. He didn't know his way back home.

"I'm lost!" cried the little boat.

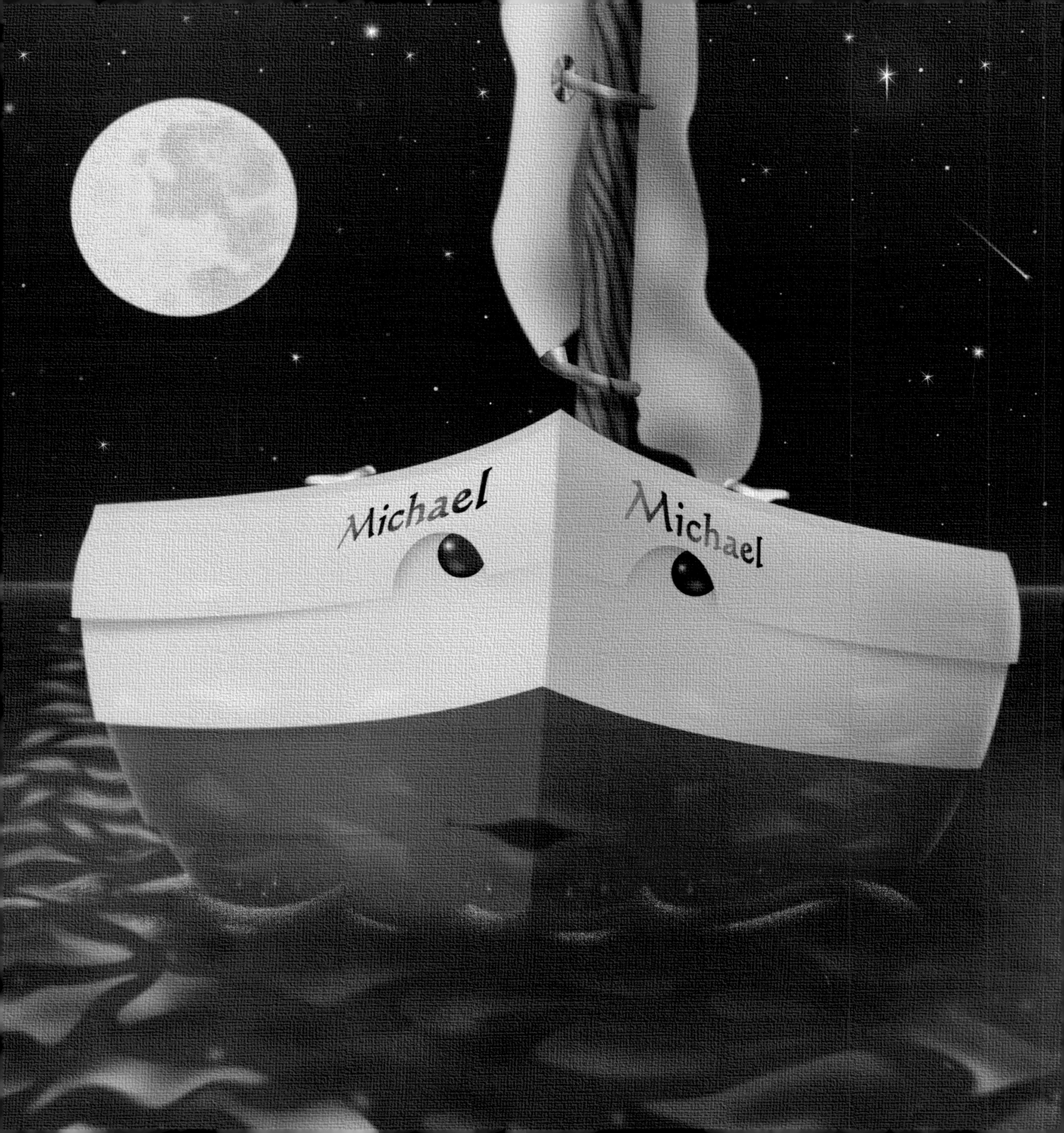
Michael
Michael

Just when the boat thought it couldn't get any worse, the wind stopped blowing. The sailboat could never remember a time when the wind did not blow.

The boat was alone in the middle of dark water and dark sky. It was night and he was lost. The little boat was scared.

"Where is the wind?" he wailed.

"I thought you didn't believe in me anymore," replied a gentle whisper.

The sailboat had not talked to the wind in a long time. Maybe he couldn't believe the wind was talking to him, or maybe he was ashamed of himself for not talking to his friend for so long. The boat didn't answer the whisper of the wind, and the wind refused to blow.

The night crept slowly past. As the dawn light broke over the horizon the boat thought to himself, "The wind will come back now. The wind always blows during the day."

The day was hot. The sea was empty. There were no waves. There was no wind. The little sailboat tried to stick his mast high up in the air in hopes of catching some wind, but there was nothing to catch.

Another scorching day crawled by slowly. There was glaring sun and dark still water, but no sign of the wind.

The next day the little sailboat was desperate to sail again. He decided to trick the wind.

"Wind?"

"Yes?" came the familiar voice.

"I believe in you!"

Immediately the wind filled his sails and the little boat began to move. The boat skimmed across the waves. Salt spray splashed high in the air. And then suddenly, the wind stopped.

"Wind, why did you stop blowing?"

"I will only blow for you if you believe in me. You wanted to trick me. I did my part. I filled your sails. Now, you know that I am real."

The wind grew silent.

The sailboat was silent too.

"If the wind is not really talking to me, then how is it filling my sails?" the little boat wondered.

"Wind?"

"Yes?"

"I believe in the river, the ocean, and the harbor. I can see them. I can't see you."

The wind puffed and filled his sails. The boat jumped into the waves. The boat sailed faster and faster skimming across the bright blue sea. Suddenly, the wind stopped blowing. The sail sagged and the boat coasted to a stop. The sea grew calm. There was silence.

"Sailboat?"

"Yes?" answered the boat.

"Did you see your sail billow out when I blew?"

"Yes," admitted the little boat.

"You may not be able to see me, but you can see what I can do. I can fill your sails and move your boat."

The little boat knew this was true. He believed, and the wind began to blow.

The little boat began to sail again. Something had changed. The bright blue sea seemed to have a little more sparkle. The salt spray felt cool and refreshing splashing against his bow. For the first time in a long time, the little boat felt like laughing.

The boat and the wind talked all day. They talked as old friends do when they haven't seen each other for a long time.

The wind puffed and sent the boat skidding across the waves.

"Yippee!" yelled the boat with delight, "I love crashing the waves and spraying the water in the air!"

When the little boat smiled the wind was happy.

The mouth of the river appeared ahead, and the two friends sailed toward home.

"You know why I love to crash the waves?"

"Of course," whistled the wind," the spray tickles!"

"It is nice to have a friend who really knows you," said the boat with a big smile.

"I know," whispered the wind.

Steve Tiller has shipwrecked many times. The last time the boat started taking on a lot of water he found himself in Atlanta. He was very familiar with the local woods, and he fixed the boat with the help of others too numerous to mention. He stopped sailing out so far, and took to trading in local waters. His crew includes Ben, Katie, Rachel, and his mom. They are of diverse size, but each does a special job that keeps the rigging straight. Steve's heart still hears the wild cry of the seagull from the deep sea.

Husband, Daddy, and "computer folk artist" **Robert Cremeans** sailed into Georgia waters from West Virginia. He learned straight sailing from his Mom and Dad. He attended CCAD and studied exploration. After sailing through Ohio, Robert anchored in Atlanta. He took on a fair maiden (and co captain) Naomi, and two small crew, Blue and Noah. The three of them help keep the sails taut, the ship shiny, and the compass in good working order.